W9-BLY-763

Making a Friend

Story by Tammi Sauer
Pictures by Alison Friend

HARPER
An Imprint of HarperCollinsPublishers

Making a Friend

 For information address HarperCollins Children's Books, a division of HarperCollins Publishers, 195 Broadway, New York, NY 10007.
www.harpercollinschildrens.com

Library of Congress Control Number: 2017913787
ISBN 978-0-06-227893-7

The artist used Photoshop and penciled scans
to create the digital illustrations for this book.
Typography by Rachel Zegar

18 19 20 21 22 SCP 10 9 8 7 6 5 4 3 2 1

First Edition

For every friend I've ever made

—T.S.

For Jill McElmurry.

Forever in the picture books you illustrated,

the landscapes you painted, and always in our hearts.

—A.F.

Beaver was good at making lots of things.

EXHIBIT A:
a lodge
EXHIBIT B:
a slide
EXHIBIT C:
stripy socks

But there was one thing he had trouble with . . .

. . . making a friend.

No matter how hard he tried—

—nothing ever went as planned.

Then one day, an idea fell from the sky.

Beaver went right to work.

Before long, Raccoon stopped by to investigate.

Fortunately,
I am **one** raccoon.
One plus **one** is **two!**

Genius!

Together, Beaver and Raccoon . . .

rolled . . .

and patted . . .

and stacked.

Then they looked things over.

Beaver and Raccoon attached sticks here and there.

Yes!
What's pizzazz?
It means
"excitement."

Ooh.
My favorite!

So Beaver and Raccoon added this and that and this and that and this and that until . . .

They made a friend!

Beaver and Raccoon admired their new friend.

Hello!
Want to play?
How do you do?
Want a raisin?

But the friend did not say “Wow” or “Thanks” or anything.

Beaver and Raccoon slumped against a nearby drift. This friend was not much of a friend at all. In fact, he seemed rather cold.

NT TO BE MY FRIEND?

Then Beaver looked at Raccoon, and Raccoon looked at Beaver.

Hey, Raccoon . . .

So, um, do you remember
a few minutes ago when
we were rolling and
patting and stacking?

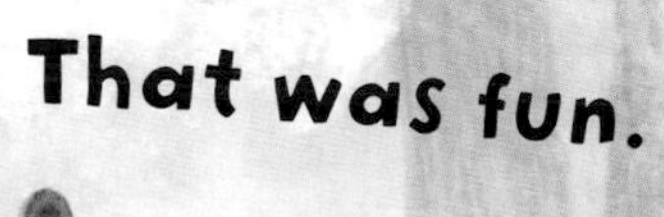

Do you remember
when we were adding
sticks and pizzazz?

I totally
LOVED that.

And remember when we
JUST became friends?

Yes!
I so remember right now!

Since then, Beaver and Raccoon have made lots of things.

I baked raisin bread.
Ooh. My favorite!

But the best thing they
made was a friend.